Being Home

A Southwestern Almanac

By Catalina Claussen

Photographs by Ajalaa Claussen

Progressive
RISING PHOENIX PRESS ®

Acknowledgments

What a joy to bring together this quirky collection of stories made possible by the oddities and eccentricities of those living in this tiny corner of New Mexico. Once again it is the support of family and friends that makes this journey possible. To my beautiful children, thank you for your vision and bringing this project to life. My daughter, Ajalaa Claussen's brilliant photography illuminates these pages, imparting to the viewer the beauty and character of the Mimbres Valley and its residents. Banyan Claussen, my son, seized the chance to design this cover, full of humor and wonder.

As always, special thanks to my writing group for encouraging me to move forward with this collection. These stories come out of my deep love for southwest New Mexico and a drive to keep story flowing when I can't figure out what to write next in my current novel. I'm continually amazed at the group's laughter and appreciation for detail. Jane Janson, your endless curiosity enlightens me. Chris Lemme, your fearless approach to writing the grit, grime, and dark underbelly of human nature never ceases to amaze me. Linda Ferrara thank you, thank you for your careful and consistent read of early drafts.

A huge thank-you to Ken Keppler at KURU Radio 89.1 FM Community Radio for teaching me about recording and learning to really listen. I appreciate you for believing in *Being Home* as a radio series. It was delightful to see your sparkly blue eyes light up with recognition as you listened patiently to early recordings. Your silver-bearded chuckles encouraged me. Decked out in your striped overalls and engineer's cap, filling the airwaves with truth, justice, and music, you are a true "irrepressible radical." And that, my friend, is the highest compliment.

To my publisher, Amanda Thrasher, at Progressive Rising Phoenix Press, I am deeply grateful for your guidance and drive. To William Speir, head of production, I so appreciate your tireless attention to detail. To my Mom, Diana Edwards, and the behind the scenes copy editors, you are amazing!

Being Home

January: Coyote Ugly

It's been a quiet week in the Mimbres Valley. The residents ride out cold-infused calm in their thick-walled adobe houses as acrid smoke from their chimneys rises and disappears into the clear blue sky. The temperature has dipped just below freezing for a week with the occasional day of forty degrees. The mother wind blows, sending clouds in to do their duty. But the sun steals their frosty ambition. So the residents are left staring at the sky, full of expectation, wondering if, when, and why it doesn't snow.

* * *

Brandon Johnson sits bolt upright on the couch fulfilling his end of the winter bargain as he battles out the flu. The sweats and chills have him whipped up in a soufflé of sickness as he hunkers down for a third day of aches and pains. A born workaholic, the illness has him wrestling the delusions and realities of running his landscaping business. He calls out to his wife.

"Say, could you be sure to send out that invoice to… to… I think it's Senator Maldonado, or was it the DA? And what about that pile of manure? That's good house warming material there. Yessir."

Since invoicing every dignitary in the community and shoveling poop into the corners of their homes is probably not the best career move, Cathie ignores him.

"I'm going to Las Cruces," she declares, setting herself a germ-free distance from Brandon on the edge of their organic cotton couch. "Need anything?" Visions of shopping malls, an indoor pool, and a bookstore dance in her head.

"All I need is you," he says dispiritedly.

Cathie sighs, cocks her head and blows a flirtatious farewell kiss.

"Bye, Daddy," Angie, his daughter, says. The front door opens and bangs shut.

While being sick has put a strain on the work week, a house emptied of the demands of women spurs Brandon forward into a day dedicated to the deeds of men.

He sets his big toe on the geothermally heated cement floor and prepares himself for a grand re-entrance into the world of men. Brandon is an investor of sorts into his twenty-year marriage to a large-breasted, lascivious, left-leaning broad. He knows that languishing in her luxuries this evening is dependent on his adherence to a don't-ask-don't-tell policy he discovered years ago. On fresh legs resembling the temerity of a newborn foal, he picks up the phone and dials John's number. "So it seems I might could come out with you for that coyote hunt after all."

Cathie Johnson and Angie are feeling light, unburdened of the concerns of men. Turning from Royal John Mine Road onto New Mexico Highway 61, their flight from the house comes to screeching halt. A fuzzy-antlered buck stands, mid-road, puzzling about his sure collision with Cathie's silver Honda Pilot. As he stares at the windshield, his thoughts about side-stepping the SUV are side-tracked by a voluptuous vixen. Cathie slams on the brakes, and Angie says, "Ooh, look at that doe, Mom. See her? Up on the hillside? She's pretty!"

The buck is startled as the grill of Cathie's Honda bumps his nose. He suppresses his instinct to run like a shrill, middle-school girl and saunters off the asphalt in the vixen's direction.

"Boys are dumb," Angie says flatly.

* * *

"Well, look who's grown some balls," John Barnum replies to Brandon on the phone. "Meet us at the Chisme. We'll gear up and go." Ah, yes, the Chisme Café and General Store, the home and heartbeat for residents of the Mimbres Valley.

Brandon is out the door in his long underwear, searching the yard for the cooler he uses to keep his camouflage gear "fresh." *Every man's got his stash*, he reasons. *Every man*. He eases the door of the straw bale shed open. By the light of the wine bottles embedded in the fibrous walls, he makes out the silhouette of his compound bow, The Bone Collector.

With the last piece of his ensemble in place, Brandon starts the engine of his 1956 Chevy Apache. Old Bessie is a modified dump truck with a sheet metal wraparound window and a carpet made from a Hudson's Bay Company woolen blanket. Years ago, Cathie insisted on installing the crushed red velvet bench seat, after claiming that bucket seats are the invention of evangelists who don't know how to keep a marriage hot. With a foolish grin on his face dipped in the memory of his bride fastened to his side and an image of the day ahead, Brandon relaxes to the seductive sounds of Sade as he points the truck in the direction of the Chisme Café.

"Hiya, John, Lester, Norman, Judd," Brandon nods to each as he enters the Chisme. Lester, a one-time mechanic, two-time veteran of foreign wars, and three-timing ex-husband, raises his iced café caramel macchiato and motions for Brandon to join them. Brandon, a little wary of those froofy coffee drinks, orders, "Café Americano black."

Grannie Max, septuagenarian barista, senses malevolence with the help of the reading glasses perched on the end of her nose. She studies Brandon's Mossy Oak garb. With fists balled up against unseen forces and set on her ample hips, she asks, "Does yer wife know about this?"

* * *

It used to be that coyotes and deer lived in perfect balance. Sadly this is no more. And the real reason that men feel it is their duty to restore this balance is it is one more way to assert their masculinity in an uncertain world *and* impress their women. But for Brandon, whose well-endowed, wanton wife has no idea that he is doing this, his motivation remains a mystery, even to himself. Why would a man want to put himself in harm's way with the possibility of winding up in a wheelchair from a stray bullet escaping the double barrels of John's shotgun?

He doesn't know the answer.

Granny Max, feeling sorry for posing such a confounding question, offers Brandon a consolation chore with his cup of coffee. "I was wondering if you would be so kind as to take down the Christmas lights before you go."

Brandon, a servant to his community, can't say no. He heads out again, enjoying the warmth of his Café Americano as it seeps into his chilled hands. So consumed with his cup of respite from the cold, he fails to notice the gallon-size iced tea bottle filled with coyote urine that Judd so faithfully collected over the last three weeks. He trips over the bottle, shattering the plastic in the cold air, while splashing his boots and camo pants with this salacious attractant.

"Ah, piss," he mutters.

Not one to let such an incident stand in his way, he ascends to the rooftop to get to work. In these frigid January days, solid footing is fleeting on tin rooftops. As Brandon unhooks the first string of red, green, and white lights, his urine-saturated cowboy boots give way. He finds himself in a twisted, tornado of holiday cheer, dangling from the highest rooftop peak, the widow's nest, of the Chisme Café. Dazed and bedazzled in strobing Christmas color, Brandon swings, raising a pungent scent of coyote into the crisp morning air.

Norman chugs down the last of his vanilla latte with chocolate sprinkles and wonders what's happened to their most junior hunting companion. His curiosity is baited by the unmistakable stench of urine in the air. Norman steps out, careful to zip his Carhart jacket up over his red long john onesie. He adjusts his earflaps to keep the wind off him for a "blasted second" while he takes full inventory of the situation.

Savoring his robust talent for stating the obvious, he inhales. On the exhalation Norman says, "Seems you got yerself in a fix." He pauses, perhaps for a dramatic effect, and then says, "Need any help there?" Now Norman's not the type to steal a man's thunder, or his DIY spirit, if you will, but he feels compelled to softly add, "Looks like you might could use some."

Brandon, up-ended and engaged in a battle against vertigo, is stunned into silent reply, punctuated by his keys, cellphone, wallet, and flask of Peppermint Schnapps that rain down on the sidewalk. Lester, Judd, and John make halting steps out on the porch, joining Norman's search for explanation.

"Well, would you looky there." What Brandon and his hunting companions miss in their focused attention on the dangling crisis at hand is the slow, silent gathering of coyotes, like back row first-timers in Sunday service, recognizing their own scent, but not their own kind.

From his vantage point, suspended and twinkling high above the rest, the sheer genius of God's plan comes into Brandon's purview. The coyotes, high on salts and their own pheromones, close in on the posse of unarmed, caffeinated men. Because in that moment, when the hunters become the hunted, balance is restored.

February: Roadside Assistants

It's been a quiet week in the Mimbres Valley out on the edge of—of *everything*. The excitement mid-week was a snowstorm that would have registered as a blip on the radar for most Rocky Mountain residents. But the Valley is the second to last stop on the southern tip of the Continental Divide Trail. A day that starts out at fifty degrees and then turns to hover just under thirty-two long enough to produce miniature flakes is an occasion for alarm among superintendents who decide the fate of hundreds of children in the county. School leaders agonize over how much snow is too much… and how much ice is too risky for the future leaders of America. Ah winter, the only season where a chilly trip to town, the one taken on this fateful snow day, can end in romantic tragic-comedy.

Cathie Johnson, English teacher, is headed home after a productive, student-free day at work. She is wary of snowflakes mingling with dirt on the surface of the road—how they drift this way and that, swirling, eddying, and finally drawing into the arroyo that trapped a 1940 Dodge Desoto in a bygone flash flood. That dry snow ripples across a tenacious ball of fluff clinging to the edge of the road. Cathie pulls into one of those rainbow-shaped drives that surround lonely mailboxes along the road. She sits, nestled in the down of her puffy jacket, and speculates whether there is life in that fluff. The dirt-speckled snow drives on, pelting the passenger door before slipping under the vehicle, crossing the road and skimming over and around the steadfast ball. Cathie cocks the driver's side door open and looks up and down the empty highway as far as she can see. She climbs down from her seat, pulls her collar closer, and closes the door behind her. In seconds, she crosses the road and squats down to examine the creature.

"For heaven's sake," Cathie says, sighing. She tries to scoop up the poor, shivering body and finds that something holds it fast.

The kitten's paws are frozen to the road.

Cathie rubs her palms together and places them over its paws.

"Mew. Mew."

While maintaining her makeshift warming pads, Cathie stares down the road. She questions why it is always empty. *Well, it isn't always empty.* She is grateful that Old Pablo Oscuro is safely behind bars. In a moment like this, he would have turned his turquoise, early 1970s Ford truck on her and the kitten—for sport. In the haze of his daily fifth of whiskey, he could sniff out vulnerability and crush a person's spirit, like the boiled eggs he stomped on when his grandchildren brought their Easter baskets for him to see.

On a day like this, when the snow and dirt can twist into any old shape, it could have conjured him, eighty years old and meaner than the devil. There's a theory among Valley residents that the reason why Pablo hasn't met his maker is because no maker will claim him.

"Mew, mew."

"It's okay, little one. We're going to make it." Cathie tucks her face deeper into her collar. She lifts her right palm and tests the frozen paw. All but two claws are unstuck. Determined to free this innocent kitten, she tries to massage the rest of his paw off the tar.

Just then, a set of lights appears, shining through the dust, snow, and gathering dark. Cathie is certain that, as her luck would have it, God has decided to come for Pablo after all. And she'll have to somehow manage to give the Almighty Pablo's forwarding address at the Grant County Detention Center while warming kitten paws off the surface of the road. *How has life become so complicated?*

A truck pulls off the side of the road and parks behind Cathie's soccer mom SUV.

The driver's side window comes down part way, enough to reveal a cowboy hat and a set of prying eyes. There seems to be some effort to open the window a little more and then a silent moment of giving up.

Finally, Cathie hears, "Howdy, stranger."

Cathie looks up across the road and sees John Barnum, the roly-poly regular at the Chisme Café who hangs out in a muddle of men over steaming lattes to suck their teeth and speculate on Sarah Palin's next career move, including whether she might consider moving in with one of them now that the presidency is out of the question. After all, those Alaska winters get people down after a while, and the Mimbres Valley is full of sunshine.

John's ten-gallon hat shades the 48-hour stubble on his chin and cheeks and rolls of extra flesh girding his neck. His baby blue eyes twinkle. He chortles and spits. "Looks like you got a problem."

John knows Cathie is the kind of gal who will walk the two miles from her house, past his house, his corral, and his cattle to the highway just to see how far two miles really is. And while Cathie isn't skinny, she isn't fat either, and that makes him nervous. Fat women are easy to read. They've got good healthy appetites—end of story. Skinny women, on the other hand, are flightier than tumbleweeds, and he doesn't want any part of them.

But Cathie is the kind of uppity gal, born in the city, who doesn't attend the Mimbres Valley Methodist on Sundays and who changes her own flat tires. One time John caught her doing an oil change in her yard on that old Toyota, and there wasn't a place in his mind to store that kind of information.

So he's not inclined to ask her if she needs help. Instead, he pauses, taking a contemplative drag on his Marlboro, while classic country pours out of his open window. After he makes a full assessment of the situation, he says, "Yep," and releases a rill of smoke into the icy air.

Cathie exhales too and nods to herself, a kind of affirmation as to why she's not a church-going woman. God. God is full of wonders that unfold regardless of where you are on Sunday. John emerges from his truck in a yellow plaid long-sleeve. His boot tips point north and south along the road as he hitches up his britches before coming across.

He strikes up a position in front of Cathie, observing her as she peels the kitten from the roadway. Whether he is conscious of it or not, he is helping Cathie by shielding her from the elements with the sheer girth of his triple extra-large chemise.

That's when Lezlie the Lesbian pulls up in her Volkswagen Rabbit held together by duct tape and an odd ritual she undertakes each time she gets in the car. Cathie stumbles over Lezlie's name in her mind. It's not that she's uncomfortable with her sexual orientation. It's just that Cathie doesn't know Lezlie's family name, so she can't readily distinguish Lezlie from Leslie, the minister's wife. Folks in the Valley have taken to calling her Lezlie the Lesbian as if that would solve matters. True, this surname of sorts does state the fact of Lezlie's appetites, but it fails to signify any other facet of her as a human being.

This conundrum has Cathie's attention as Lezlie pulls off the road and into the rainbow driveway next to the lonely mailbox that now has three visitors. Lezlie fairly bounces from her car.

She calls out over the rattle of her engine, "Need any help?"

* * *

In a jaunty juxtaposition with John, Lezlie's toes brim out of her Birkenstocks while the wind sends fresh waves of snow and dirt rippling across them. John's worn boots sag under his weight, threatening to burst at the seams. From her prostrate vision of these two unlikely foot soldiers, Cathie senses an enigmatic shift.

Another truck comes barreling down the road in their direction, no headlights, no warning just as Cathie pries the last paw off the asphalt and springs to her feet. The engine whines with its increasing speed. But there's no time.

Out of instinct and reminiscent of the Rapture, John swoops Lezlie and Cathie into his arms. He spares them the tribulations of ice cream and frozen fish so often found in the recesses of the Schwan man's refrigerated step-van. Suspended in John's sudden selfless gesture, Cathie's sensitive nose picks up on Lezlie's sandalwood beads and Dr. Bronner's lavender soap mixed with John's tobacco, beer, Fruit Loops and unmistakable couch potato sweat.

In that moment, Cathie senses a distinct dimension of something bigger than her—a divine design, if you will. *What kind of world it would be if there were kittens frozen to the roadside everywhere, say every 100 feet, so others might have the chance to share a moment just like this?* Then she thinks better of it. You can't have an outreach program for everything.

The truck passes. John holds them all a bit longer than he should.

"Mew, mew."

He loosens his grip, realizing he may have squished the kitten and blasted skinny Lezlie right out of her shoes. He considers the women clutched in his arms for a moment, before easing them back down on the roadside. Cathie, in an attempt to recover, tucks the kitten into the folds of her jacket while Lezlie's Volkswagen Rabbit rattles on in the background.

There's something about the silence among them in that split second that compels them to consider the enormity of what just happened and struggle with where to put that information. With their feet firmly returned to the ground, they all step back, away from the edge of the arroyo where the 1940 Desoto took its final plunge.

John's manner is reverent. He half expects the experience to be followed by a few trays of green chile enchiladas, dirty rice, and black beans accompanied by a cup of the weak church coffee served in a Styrofoam cup. His stomach growls with anticipation.

Instead, he witnesses Lezlie's silent car ritual that includes a number of garrulous gestures and methodic mudras. Cathie fumbles a "thanks" through the unrelenting storm that has just become a little colder in contrast to the unexpected warmth of their shared embrace.

March: Laissez-Faire

It's been a tempestuous day in the Mimbres Valley.

The wireless weathermen seem to have the 10-day forecast set on repeat. *Sunny and 70, no precipitation*. It's as if the term wireless has gone to their heads. No strings attached, laissez-faire, weathermen thriving in a free-market society where few will know that the forecast is a facsimile of a sham carried out by 'experts' in far-flung states like Minnesota, where meteorologists toy with temperature predictions and throw in a precipitate teaser that is nothing short of non-committal when one enters "10 percent chance of rain."

So you see, the residents of the Valley are unprepared for the snowstorm that descends upon them one morning in late March.

The snow itself fell like granules of pulverized Styrofoam coffee cups, herded into the corners of the yard, but never packing down like a traditional snow drift ought to. That would be too easy.

"Daddy, I told you I need a woobie," Angie declares, surveying the damage done to the greenhouses. Plastic sheeting, shredded and torn, has come unhinged from the PVC framework. Sudden gusts claw at the wreckage, whipping the remains in the air. "It would keep the wind off me just like yours," she says surveying the black sturdy canvas of his coveralls.

The two of them stand there, coffees in hand. His is black, no cream no sugar. And hers is an exact replica of her mother's, iced, enough cream to turn the mixture light caramel color, and three heaping teaspoons of sugar because life should be sweet, especially in a weather crisis. Brandon exhales a laugh.

"I know, girl. The store doesn't stock them in your size." He turns up his corduroy collar against the driving wind and wipes away God's uncertain snow from his moustache and goatee. They stand there in silence watching gusts batter the greenhouse plastic, sending it hither and yon.

With no woobie to call her own, Angela slides her free hand into the pocket of her father's. Her fingers find lint, dirt, a quarter, and a pair of cigarette butts used to plug his ears when he works with heavy equipment. *A man's pocket*, she thinks.

Angela tries to think of something to change the subject, something to keep her father's mind off the hours of labor in the greenhouse gardens that might go to waste in the next freeze, which could be as early as tonight.

Then her mind fixes on a few therapeutic sweet nothings as the sting of the snow nips their cheeks. "This week," she says, "at school, my teacher made us build triangles out of split peas and spaghetti noodles. Then we calculated how many desks we could fit into our classroom from floor to ceiling. I forgot what it's called and oh at lunch I took a poll. We heard on the news that the Supreme Court justices are trying to figure out if gay people should be married or something. So I asked around. And you know what they said, Daddy? Daddy?"

She realizes she's on a fifth grade ramble and suddenly thinks better of it.

Sinking into the silence that is a part of being with him, Angie considers "The Art of Conversation," one in a million lectures provided by her mother, an English major from a small liberal arts college in the Pacific Northwest. She always says it's important to pause and perhaps ask your listener a question to keep them engaged.

So, Angela asks again, "You know what they said?"

Brandon, sips on his black coffee, now growing decidedly cold, and considers what could be done to shore up the greenhouses. But the wind is a force to contend with, and he isn't so sure that the struggle will pay off.

"Hunh?" he says, keeping part of an ear trained on his daughter's words.

Angela, proud of herself for getting his attention, prattles on. "Well, some of them, my friends anyway, say that they are for it. And some of them say they aren't. I can't understand how you could be against gay marriage. I just don't get people." Angela pulls her hand from her dad's woobie to emphasize her point with a tap to her temple. She finds herself getting whipped up over the issue and lapses into silence. Then she resettles her hand in his pocket.

Brandon thinks she's been spending too much time with her mother, listening to that AM liberal radio station that calls itself unbiased news coverage. The same station forecasted Sunday night's weather as "Cloudy with a chance of meteors."

Brandon shakes his head. A feller has but a few choices of radio stations in the country, a fact of life he has come to accept. But now look at her, his daughter, a veritable heretic of liberal politics.

Then he realizes, too late, that he is saying some of this out loud.

He stops, reaches into the pocket of his coveralls and finds lint, dirt, a quarter, and cigarette butts to protect his ears from loud noises and his daughter's hand, which he holds in his. He eyes the male and female couplings of the PVC pipes previously arced into a greenhouse framework, now forced apart in the wind and shrugs.

It's his turn to change the subject. But he doesn't get a chance. The bracing chill spurs him into action.

"Well, let's get pickin'," he says. "We'll give the neighbors one last taste of the good life before we have to start over."

April: Hot Wheels

It's been a disquieting week in the Mimbres Valley as the April winds stir up dust and pollen, smearing the clear blue sky. The gusts rattle roof tins enough to remind Grannie Max of the corrugated metal John promised to tack down *last* spring.

Clair LaBelle flexes her fingers. She enjoys the feeling of a good knuckle crack beneath her driving gloves. There is something invigorating about the spring zephyrs running between her fingers as she speeds along the shoulder of the highway in her new wheelchair.

Making her way across the uneven pavement, she imagines being flanked by like-minded, irrepressible radicals, including bisexual tricyclists, trilingual tandem riders, and the solo white-bearded unicyclist she once saw pedaling effortlessly uphill in his racing tights.

Clair makes a beeline for the Chisme Café and General Store with her auburn feathered hair, hawk-billed nose set slightly left of center and her body tilted forward, testing her overall aerodynamics.

Clair is unmarried, disabled, and has been living with her father all these years after her mother died of cancer. She keeps company with an ageless former mariachi artist turned painter and mason to keep the beer flowing, the women happy, and the old ones in Durango, Mexico proud. These character traits set her apart from the typical Chisme clientele. But she can work up a good old-fashioned grievance with the best of them, which makes her the toast of the Chisme kaffeeklatch.

"Mornin'," Grannie Max greets Clair as she tops the ADA certified ramp leading up to the general store.

Clair grunts in reply. The last ten feet of the ramp make her question how many members of the American Disabilities Act Committee or Commission, or whatever, are actually disabled. She quashes the impulse to berate the institution since she and Grannie have been over it a few times before.

Grannie Max isn't about to leave the comfort of the "raggedy ass" rocker that exposes a patch of her flowered housedress through the worn wicker seat. The way she figures it, she has already risked social suicide by leaving her tin-rattling perch for the comfort of Doc's general store in such a hurry that she neglected to get dressed properly. So she isn't about to get tangled up in someone else's fight with the government. *Besides*, she tells herself, *how will anybody ever learn that life is hard if you're always babying folks through it. Tough love. That's what they call it, nowadays, tough love.*

Clair finally crests the ramp, wipes sweat from her brow, and rolls to a stop next to Grannie's chair. The silence that follows is just short of a religious experience as they listen to the wind roll in and out, tossing the vivid green-tipped willows this way and that.

"I'm on the run," Clair announces to Grannie, whose deep breaths have eased her into a stupor where her eyelids are drawn half-shut against the elements. Grannie's the oldest upstart the Valley's ever known and Clair knows her confidence will be admired and understood by a woman of her caliber. Grannie always says there's no such thing as can't. She also says, "There's 'I'm too lazy,' 'I'm not up to the task,' and 'This goddam so-and-so is in my way.' But there's no such thing as *can't*."

Grannie moves to run the fingers of both hands through her shorn hair and lets a grin of recognition spread across her face. Her chest rises and falls pleasantly, letting the black-rimmed, cat-eyed reading glasses resting against her chest catch a ray of the morning light in the jewels at the temples.

"From the law?" Grannie asks exhaling. Her interest is piqued, but not enough to open her eyes all the way.

"Nope," Clair says, stretching her wrists.

"Mornin'," John says, making his way up on the porch. He collects himself from the strain it takes to top the last step and lets out a satisfied breath. He notices Grannie Max cooled out on the rocker and tips his hat in Clair's direction.

"*To* them," Clair says.

"Come again?" Grannie asks.

"You heard me," Clair says, gathering her venom. "I'm runnin' *to* the law."

Grannie lets out a one-syllable giggle and thinks about what she saw last week. Filiberto Aguilera, Clair's topless part-time lover, was swept up in an intoxicating ukulele solo in Janis's budding cactus garden. His tanned, taut skin pressed against the waistband of his Fruit of the Looms was notable and certainly timeless if you go for that kind of thing.

She lets out a sigh. And, still sticking to her tough love philosophy, she finally says, "You can't legislate love."

Her comment hangs in the air and seems unfinished, like the Valentine's Day pillow she started to embroider one year for her long-time companion, Rosemary, and then she thought better of it.

Grannie adds a comment that she thinks makes her sound wise to life's trials in a general sense, nothing too personal, and she says, "You certainly can't enforce it either. It just is."

She peeks out from under her left eyelid to see if Clair is listening in the shrill silence.

She is.

Grannie's words seem to stop Clair in her tracks. Grannie doesn't seem to know one way or another what is making Clair run *to* the law. So she sits back and waits for the answer to come.

Doc's voice drifts through the air and out through the fiberglass screen in the window above Grannie's head as he shares in the counsel of men with John.

"You say you're engaged are you?"

Then the conversation takes a pause that often accompanies confusion.

"Her name's Aubrey," John says. You can hear his satisfied smile spreading across his face.

Doc's memory for names and faces is remarkable and is one of the reasons why his store prospers this far out in the middle of nothing. You feel like a Hollywood star each time the cowbells ring on the door to announce your arrival. He knows your name and the names of your kinfolks and maybe just a bit too much about the goings on in your world, enough to add a certain je-ne-sais-quoi to the conversation. So when John announces his forthcoming nuptials, Doc says, "I thought her name was Ellie."

"It was," John says matter-of-factly. "It was." And that was all he had to say about that.

John gathers the top of his paper sack in one hand. The brown paper rustles and bristles against his calloused fingertips.

"You tell Julie, I say hi," Doc says. "And tell her she owes me some sweeping up for last week's Tootsie Pop."

"I will," John chuckles. Julie, John's daughter, is a well-seasoned kleptomaniac, a practice that holds both their interests and keeps her delightfully conscripted to doing Doc's bidding.

Doc's words are his version of a well-child check since this is the third time in just as many weeks that he's sold John some liquor on the Lord's day and every day in between. And he didn't like hearing the name of a woman he had no memory of either.

The screen door slaps behind John as he makes another grand entrance on the porch. Grannie Max hasn't moved yet and has no intention of moving.

"Ladies," John says more for Clair's benefit than anyone else's.

Clair watches John descend the stairs and jam his thumb in the handle of the driver's side door to release the latch. A sudden gust swirls dried manure, hay, and grit from the truck bed and carries it off into the ether. The gust knocks something loose in Clair. She glimpses herself free of the limitations of her aching hands. She sees herself take flight, tasting freedom, a hot wind, if you will, that she has never known.

As John loads his paper sack in the cab of his truck and busies himself collecting trash launched from the driver's side door, Clair descends the ramp, gathering gumption for her next big feat. Yes, she will embody a metaphor for a misguided belief that she has held so dear. She will prove that men can set you free. She flexes her driving gloves again, contemplating how they might hold up on frayed rope that hangs listlessly off the trailer hitch of John's truck. Chasing after trash in the parking lot comes to a sudden end, and John launches himself into the driver's seat.

Clair wants to know what it feels like to play ukulele for budding cacti and ride fearlessly uphill on countless wheels. She just has to know. John's twin tail pipes shroud her in exhaust and that's why Grannie Max doesn't see her at first. The noise of John's engine forces her eyes open. At first, Grannie thinks Clair went inside to soothe herself with Doc's famous cappuccino ice cream like most sensible women in the Valley. But, she quickly realizes this isn't the case when Doc bursts through the screen door.

"Good land," he exhales, showing his Georgia roots in a single expression. "Why would she go off an' do such a thing?"

Grannie's vision clears. She spies Clair in a foreboding pose at the rear of John's dually. She exhales, as there is not much else a person can do. Then she thinks of something she read in one of her sci-fi books written by a Mr. Heinlein, "Women and cats will do as they please, and men and dogs should relax and get used to the idea."

John puts the truck in drive. Focused on the paper sack in the passenger seat and the immensely short drive home, he is unaware of the unsuspecting, and perhaps ill-fated rider, taking up the reins dangling from his trailer ball. Clair tests her grip on the tattered rope and twines her driving gloves twice its tethers. She leans back in her chair and tips herself up on the back wheels. In this moment, like no moment before, she feels as if her liaison with a muscular mariachi, her downtrodden dad, and her belief in holding one's stars in one's hands have all come to the fore.

Doc races into the store and dials Sheriff Miles. He finds he hasn't the words to explain it. So he says simply, "You better come have a look-see."

From her perch on the front porch Grannie Max watches the scene unfold. Clair, unbridled and unabashedly free, explodes from the starting gates of the parking lot, pops up onto a freshly oiled section of the road, and, with the help of her reins tethered to an eight cylinder engine producing 230 horsepower and 330-pound feet of torque, charges toward the warm embrace of the law.

Freedom never tasted so good.

It's been a quiet week in the Mimbres Valley. Residents hold their collective breath in a communal prayer against the retreating forces of hoarfrost and rime. Our Lord in heaven, hallowed be thy name, thy kingdom will come undone on earth if Leslie's loquats, John's freestone peaches, and Grannie Max's pinot noir patch suffer a pistil-punishing chill. Give us this day. Any gardener worth his salt in the Valley knows frost can philander the filigree of sugar peas, cavort with cabbages and cucumbers, and taint tomatoes any time between September 15 and May 15. And as the sun crests the ridge of the Black Range Mountains on the sixteenth day in May with nary a nip on Eddie Munoz's pistachio orchard, the denizens collectively exhale.

At ten minutes to noon on the porch of the Chisme Café and General Store, Filiberto Aguilera reclines against the cool milk-chocolate adobe wall. Shaded by the tin and *viga* awning he sucks on a *tamarindo*, enjoying the sweet, salty, and piquante chile flavors as they roll across his tongue. He pulls the sucker from his lips, grateful that Sundays allow a man the opportunity to ponder the voluptuous vista laid out before him. Across the road, twin peaks rise from the prairie. The peaks softened with grasses, mounded, full-bodied, and tasseled with a pair of one-seed juniper trees perched on the precipices. And from the cleavage formed by these two bodacious bluffs, an admirer can witness the wind caress the umbered grasses that form the midline down the center of *la tierra*'s midriff heath, pierced with the tin roof of the Mennonite bakery that shimmers like a cubic zirconia in the morning sun.

Filiberto has pondered asking the other men what they see when they look out across the road. But then he's thought better of it. Enjoying the company of his private *chiquita*. Filiberto pops the sucker back in his mouth, savoring the texture of the tamarind pulp that soothes his soul as the minutes melt away. In New Mexico a man's first communion with bottled spirits isn't until noon. But that's not too much of an imposition for Filiberto when the view is this golden.

"Good morning," Mennonite Mary offers. She flounces up the steps swathed in the blue billowing skirts of her calico dress, a white apron, and a dust cap, tied in a wide bow below her chin. She is flanked by her nine children, while cradling the tenth in her arms. In a moment of quiet panic, Filiberto rifles through his inner closet for something to shield Mary and her brood from his incendiary thoughts. Precious seconds pass as his mind comes up empty. He reels, in the lurid vision of *la tierra* in contrast to the Madonna with children before him, and blinks. As his panic subsides, he is reminded why it is important for man to be alone with his thoughts.

"Buenos días," he says, praying that the sounds of his home country will snap him back into the ways of proper Catholic men. He could use that kind of guidance about now.

Mary pauses, hoping to hear a morsel of news from the world outside her own. It's not that she doesn't enjoy being a mother in service to Jesus Christ, raising herself and her family above the shackles of nationalism, racism, and materialism, living life simply. But from time to time, a tidbit of salacious gossip would be a refreshing change of pace. At last Saturday's farmer's market, barricaded behind baked goods, Mary overheard Grannie Max's tale of Filiberto in his Fruit of the Looms, whipped up in song following a particularly satisfying encounter with Janis and her spiny succulents. And as Mary scans Filiberto's tanned chiseled features, dark goatee with a dash of salt, and lithe body spattered with interior satin latex, she hopes that somehow being this close to Filiberto might warrant her a morsel of his glory. Then Mary realizes, too late, that she's staring at him.

Filiberto smiles respectfully and nods as she gathers herself up in her bonnet and leads her children into the store. He watches them pass in alphabetical birth order, boy-girl, boy-girl, each knowing their place in the flock. There's Abel, the good shepherd; Bithiah, the daughter of God; Cain, Mother Mary's assurance for a good sibling rivalry; Deborah, the bee in everyone's bonnet; Emmet, charged with telling the truth; Faith; Gabriel, the angel; Hope; Isaiah, the salvation of the lord; and baby Jedidiah, a.k.a. friend of God. No pressure there. Once the cast of the Old Testament clears the porch, Filiberto settles in for a few more cherished moments with his beloved.

But something is amiss.

A spark, a flare, a rising glow. He bears witnesses to the conflagration of his thoughts. A flash of lightning generated by a shiftless sun shower licks the bare crest of the hill on the left, setting a serpentine blaze in motion, spilling down the delectable divot between the two hills, tracing the supple, shadowed grasses of her midline.

Just when Filiberto feels he might be alone with his thoughts at last, a moment where he might discern the real from the surreal, Byron Johnson, sixteen, sporting a blond Justin Bieber coiffure plunks himself down next to Filiberto on the cooler. Byron clutches his longboard and two cold sodas. He gazes ahead, his eyes follow the hilly contours, admiring the silhouette of the golden mounds. He is a young man gifted with the sight. He hands Filiberto a cream soda, froth rising up the bottleneck of the freshly popped top. Byron turns to Filiberto and says, "Dude… that's awesome." He clinks his bottle with Filiberto's, and washes his remarks down with a swig of his own lime sherbet brew.

June: Azul Ilimitado

"It's been an exiguous week in the Mimbres Valley." Grannie Max exhales as she settles into her rattan settee on the front porch and considers the persistent azure sky. She smiles to herself and tries not to make eye contact with her new friend as she tries out Merriam-Webster's word of the day, *exiguous, exiguous*. It could roll off your tongue after a while, if a person is persistent.

Eddie Munoz settles into the recliner next to her. He tries not to sit too far back in the cushions *'Cause Grannie's a good looking, sturdy woman for her age,'* he thinks, and he might throw his chances with her if she notices that his feet don't quite touch the porch floorboards.

College was something that Grannie or Maxine DeNeuve, as she was known then, missed out on, a place with stained glass windows and vaulted ceilings where words like exiguous flowed effortlessly through the air. It's a place where a person could learn to describe just about anything, which probably would make folks around here a little nervous. And, you might could earn a few names in the community like uppity and other words that Grannie can't think of at the moment.

She turns to consider her seated guest. Grannie realizes she is being rude to what her mother would call a "gentleman caller" by getting lost in her own thoughts. She has been alone a great deal lately and entertains herself just fine. But then, she thinks, maybe she should be sociable. Pastor Rick, the new energetic, or maybe the word is *frenetic*, pastor at church challenged his flock to do so after all. "Be sociable," he said. "Two are better than one." *This is for you, Pastor Rick*.

Grannie goes back to fighting with her mother in her head. Technically, Eddie isn't a gentleman caller. He isn't in the house, and the only thing she notices that is gentlemanly about him is the way he rides the edge of her comfy chair. He chooses to perch on the outer limit of the kaleidoscope mango, lime, and sea-green poly-canvas cushion fabric, keeping his size sevens firmly rooted to the porch planks. Looking through the generous gap he leaves between the backrest and his ramrod posture, Grannie observes the thirsty blades of corn pushing up through the dirt in the side yard.

"Inadequate," she says out of the gathering blue.

Eddie jumps at her words. Too late, Granny realizes she has said a remark one should never utter to a man, especially on a first encounter.

"That's what exiguous means," she says in an emollient tone.

Eddie relaxes some. He wonders why words are hard to come by at a moment like this. They had been his allies in English and in Spanish. And, oh the things he could say to a woman in Spanish, but not on a first encounter. So, he turns to a safe subject, one upon which the residents of the

Mimbres Valley have built homes and raised cattle—the weather.

"You said it," he says, smiling some. "But we've never seen such an exiguous year as this." He, too, stares out at the *azul ilimitado*. A little coyote grin tugs at the edge of his lips, but he doesn't let Grannie Max in on the joke. Instead, he decides two can play her game.

A sudden gust seems to pick Eddie up, along with the dust and the tumbleweeds that never did come to a final resting place after last summer. The wind carries him off into a story, into another spell of remembrance that takes hold of him often since his eightieth *cumpleaños*. The tales are often accompanied by the *guitarra* he hears in his head, a wondrous riffle of strings riding the air. It's the same series of notes he has been teaching his granddaughters. *What are you doing?* He could hear his son say, as he tried to show the girls the way to hold the strings, just so, for a wandering song. And the question reminds him to come back.

He turns to Grannie Max, and he says, "You remember the good years? During the War?"

He doesn't wait for her to answer. He sees the rise and fall of her breath as he eases her into the story.

"I remember those years as if it were yesterday. Sometimes I wake up at three a.m. like I'm fourteen again, and old man Schadel will be mad at me if I'm late to work at the bakery. The community relied on us to make the cookies, the cakes, the pies, and the breads."

Grannie savors his talk. She revels in his Cs, crisp and buttery, the way he carefully pronounces each one as he nibbles at words like "cookies" and "cakes."

"Marjorie would pack the cookies by the dozen, six and six in each row."

Grannie loves the way he hangs on his Rs, too, when he says, "Marjorie." And she suddenly wishes she had Rs in her name. Then Eddie pauses and gives a quick laugh as if Grannie had been there, too, as if she can see what he can against the blue. "And the police would come with the teachers and the judge, trading us coffee and books for the sweets and the breads. Remember? Those were the good times. There was no money then. We didn't need it."

By this time Grannie is with him, and Eddie doesn't need to check on her. "There was water, too," he says, coming around to the original point that linked their thoughts. "A lot of it. I used to cross the Big Ditch, before there were bridges. My big brother was never afraid of the water. He used to call me out, 'Come on, Eddie, be a man. Jump the *piedras*. But you better not miss any,' he'd say."

Grannie Max imagines him soaked through and through in his baker's hat and apron. The puff of his hat deflated against the rising water, his apron sullied by debris and dust that could never settle in the persistent dry, nor in the flashing waters. She resists the impulse to sweep Eddie up, away from flash flood danger, and she realizes that maybe her own exiguous mind is losing a sense of reality. *You get to be a certain age*, she hears herself counsel, *and all of it is real*. She leans back against the cushions and considers the unsettling nature of the dust, the tumbleweeds, and the business of getting old.

Yep, she thinks, as she tastes the dust of her girlhood home in the Oklahoma flats, *Eddie's right. They were the good times. We had each other then.* The breeze gnaws at the edges of the tin on her roof, and it reminds her of how little she had to eat then. It reminds her of how luxuries like going into stained glass buildings to learn elevated speech among elevated rafters were certainly out of reach.

Then, Eddie says, "I tell that story to my children, my grandchildren, and my great grandchildren. But, they never believe me."

"I never would have believed it either," she sighs. "Unless, I lived it."

She returns from the blue to consider her companion. Eddie sits resting in his chair back. From his newly reclined position, his feet swing free of the floorboards. Grannie Max grins a wide gap-toothed grin and laughs, letting it roll her belly as it pleases.

July: Baby You're a Firework

It's been a sizzling week in the Mimbres Valley. Today, the annual rains make their way across the mountains and foothills, putting out the month long wildfire that has kept Effegenia De la O's grandsons on high alert and occupied them with a long list of chores. They cleared the grasses and brush from around the perennial plastic nativity scene, the faded Santa Claus, and a wide assortment of woodland creatures. And, once the brush was cleared, there was the hosing down of the ornaments and watering of the driveway, and, well, let's just say the De la O's are a busy people.

There's speculation that this rain is not "the rain." It's more like a foreign invasion of moisture, an imposter cyclical rain that folks should be wary of.

"They're sayin' it's coming off the Gulf of Mexico," John says confidentially this morning, sitting back against the shiny red vinyl of his booth at the Chisme Café. CaryAnn, the waitress, fills his coffee cup. Then he adds, "There's no border wall tall enough to hold it off."

Jesus "Chuy" Montoya, John's right-hand man and long-time roping partner who bought John's place years ago and lets him stay in his trailer out back because he has no other place to go adds, "It's a hurricane, blowing moisture up our way."

CaryAnn eyes Jesus with particular interest this morning. His cowboy hat is steamed to perfection. The top buttons open on his western shirt, giving her a taste of his light caramel complexion, are a distraction. CaryAnn has heard the kind of rumor she likes to hear about Chuy, so she slowly refills his cup with a flourish and final expert flick of her wrist. To her disappointment, he doesn't seem to notice. So, she tries another angle.

Setting the coffee pot down on the flecked laminate tabletop, she fixes imaginary strands of hair that have escaped her up-do. In a fit of liberal talk she says, "Well, I don't much care where the rain comes from as long as it makes the place wet." Chuy exhales and raises his eyebrows at John—enough said.

Cathie Johnson shifts in the booth next to John's. The talk seems a little racy this morning in front of the children, but she's grateful for the Mexican rain too, cooling the fire and inspiring such open-mindedness towards our neighbors to the south. "Thought we'd go to town today and watch the fireworks with Grandma and Grandpa." No one says much with their mouths full of the Patriot special, waffles topped with red and blue berries doused in Wonder Whip.

* * *

The advantage of country living is folks know they're entitled to their opinions. These opinions may be found on hand-painted signs fixed to fence posts declaring the evils of Obama, or in the flagpole-raised, colorfast image of the planet floating in the breeze.

Long-time residents know, too, that making peace with one another is in the best interest of all. Take Cathie Johnson's parents for an example. Cathie's mom, a retired special education teacher, calls herself a traditional Tea Party Democrat. Her dad claims he's a moderate Republican. Over the years they've made their peace with it. All year long her dad announces his opinions in the parlor from behind the pages of the newspaper, while her mom lets agreeable or disagreeable noises issue from her lips. It's just enough for him to *know* she's listening.

On election day, her mom bakes several cherry, blueberry, and banana cream pies. She borrows Mennonite Mary's extra-long Dodge van to transport many of the tea-loving, pie-eating elderly of the neighborhood to the senior citizen's center which doubles as a polling place. However, Cathie's dad never quite seems to make it to the polls. And her mom never gets around to reminding him.

It's dusk and after a roast chicken, mashed potatoes, and green beans dinner, Cathie's mom has laid out cherry, blueberry, and banana cream pies for the family.

"Well, now, here's the way I see it," her dad says between mouthfuls of cherry pie à la mode. "Course your mother will disagree with me." He sends a little spark her way just to make sure she's listening. She shakes her head as she prepares to put the vanilla ice cream back in the freezer. "Every year it's the same thing. But what it comes down to is letting people do what they do best." Cathie's dad always starts this way, one piece at a time. It must be some kind of bygone rhetorical strategy. The idea is something like keep your audience guessing about the topic of your speech until the last line.

The family wanders outside and settles into lawn chairs placed strategically on a high spot, facing south. The rustle of raven feathers up in the Arizona cypress catches Angie's attention for a moment. Brandon, a closet moderate Republican himself, sits closest to Cathie's dad. Cathie, with her portable liberal soapbox, settles in next to her mother. The children are strung out between them.

Her dad picks up his line of argument, "Every year we don't know if there's going to be a fireworks display, or not. And every year the show goes on anyway. They start late, and then when they do get going, the fireworks have a hard time clearing the trees enough for us to see them. I know they're shooting from the highest point around, but I still say they could do better."

Cathie's dad sets his pie down a moment and lets Franklin, as in Franklin Delano Roosevelt, the grey, green-eyed, long-haired tabby, pick up his leavings. Franklin is one to keep an eye on. He adores the children but is a menacing presence to small woodland creatures. A light breeze picks up and because there is not much else to do while waiting for the display to start, the family listens for the rest of Cathie's dad's position.

He settles back in his seat and says, "So, I say let the inmates of the Grant County Detention Center do some community service. Take the boy who set the music store on fire, for instance. He had two-thirds of that store up in flames before the fire department could touch it. And those punks who burned down Penny Park, they've got what it takes."

He punctuates the sentence with a fist pump. And then goes on to say, "With these boys, the fireworks display would be on time and big enough for the *whole* county." He pauses to glance at Cathie's mom, who has the youngest grandchild in her lap. Franklin is lapping up the last of their ice cream, too, as light fades from the sky.

His talk circles back, and he says, "Least Restrictive Environment." He grins, applauding himself for his use of special education teacher-talk. "That's what you and Cathie always talk about." He pauses one more time to gauge how hot the water is with his bride and then goes on. "But, just imagine what that could mean for inmates. Take that vice and turn it into a virtue for all of us."

Cathie watches as a smile spreads across her mom's face in the dying light. She says nothing to her husband of forty years. She doesn't need to. She saves her arguments for the ladies at tea enjoying red, white, and blue pies by the mouthful. She pulls her granddaughter closer and kisses her hair as the first firework, barely visible above the tree line, bursts in the night sky.

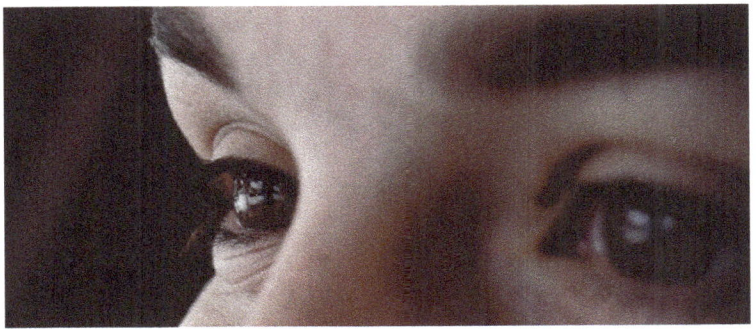

August: Three Sheets to the Wind

It's been a quiet week in the Mimbres Valley. A little too quiet. Effegenia De la O sits on the front porch of her double-wide trailer, inhaling deeply from her Virgin Slim cigarette while perusing the pages of *Glamorous Gal Magazine* and keeping a watchful eye on the mailbox. An early morning hot wind teases the lacy edge of her tap pants. She shudders with the sudden movement and draws her silk kimono closer in an effort to protect her abundant form from the elements. According to the latest magazines, Effie possesses a veritable cornucopia of a figure. She is pear-shaped—or was it apple?—with a muffin top that is sure to satisfy the appetites of a lucky man.

For Effie, it's not just any man. It's Innocencio LeBrawn. He's a tall, cool drink of water, a.k.a. the postmaster, who on any given Saturday can be found *hand* delivering the mail. There is something about a man in uniform—that dark blue stripe on permanent press denim polyester—that rattles her cupboard doors. Effie takes the last drag on her cigarette to cool her engine. Exhaling, she dabs it out in the ashtray. Moments later, she considers the remains of her "Untamed Tempest" lip stain on the filter paper. She checks the time. Effie sighs, pulls another tall, slender cigarette from the box, and places it between her lips. She grabs the carton of kitchen matches, withdraws a matchstick, and prepares to strike.

* * *

Across the fence, Mennonite Mary inhales, relishing the heady scent of the verdant landscape. Her eyes scan the once withered vegetation in the hills, giving glory to God in the highest. At the clothesline, she smooths her palm across the flats of her starched white 200 thread count, percale bed sheets and pins them in place, one by one. And just as Mary's meditation on the unfathomable providence of God's will "on earth as it is in heaven" builds to a crescendo, an errant breeze snaps at the florid edge of Ms. De la O's jacquard bedclothes. Mary, jarred from her morning worship by 800 thread count sateen sheets wonders. Her curiosity wends the short distance, betwixt the bed sheets, across the deer fencing, and rests with a shy gaze on Effie in her baby doll pajamas.

* * *

Still aloft in her outdoor boudoir, Effegenia is at a loss. Her cigarette lolls precariously from her lips, the tobacco remains unquenched by fire. She draws the third match tip across the gritty igniter and hopes. The tip sparks just as the matchstick escapes her fingers and disappears between two wooden slats.

"*Ay dios mio,*" she mutters.

Effie descends the porch stairs in pink-feathered slippers, knowing time is of the essence. She makes her way around the backside of the porch. She bends over and works to pull the lattice skirting free, two cheeks to the wind.

* * *

Mennonite Mary chides herself. Awakened at the sight of Effie's flesh, but unable to avert her gaze, she begins. "Romans 8:1 There is, therefore, no condemnation to them which are in Christ Jesus, who walk not after the flesh, but after the Spirit." But it's not enough. The verse fails to turn her head.

* * *

While the rest of the Valley received its rightful portion of monsoon rain, the brittle grasses under Effigenia's porch have been left wanting. The match bears a spark that is enough, just enough, to start a trickle of fire between Effie's legs. What was once a blazing rivulet along the earth's surface builds to Biblical proportions, the kind that the citizens of Sodom and Gomorrah could not hold back, consuming the space between Effie and Mary. Mary, powerless under the weight of her curiosity, looks on. Effie is caught in God's unfathomable chastisement, that some might call *correction,* while others might call it Old Testament tribulation.

In any case, Mother Mary full of Grace stands frozen, expectant in God's glory, three sheets to the wind.

Catalina Claussen

September: Enough

There's a certain pernicious piquant, a maladroit musing, if you will, that has settled in and among the residents of the Mimbres Valley this morning. It's a kind of odor, surreptitiously twinned with the scent of charred green chile that makes a person believe they are immune and immutable to outside forces.

On this, this second day of sixth grade with Mrs. Johnson in room 206, Ernesto Puro Corazon a.k.a. Nesto, sits in the driver's seat. It is not his first time. His *abuelita* Connie, née Inmaculada Concepción, sits in the passenger seat. Nesto adjusts the steering wheel, the mirrors, checks the wiper blades, and is satisfied. He turns to Connie and considers. Ernesto isn't totally certain that Connie knows or understands the intricacies of daily life outside of the hook and purl of her knitting *proyectos,* but he needs her. He needs her and that, he tells himself, is *suficiente.* Enough.

* * *

Cathie Johnson stands on the edge. It is the second of five days of morning parking lot duty, and she wonders where summer has gone. Clutching her caramel latte with extra whip, she curls her toes over the curb, admiring the results of her final summer pedicure, an opalescent purple polish with daisy embellishments adorning the big toenails. She prides herself in pushing the limits of teacher dress code, eschewing drugstore flip-flops for flowered leather, open-back sandals. Her pedal pusher pants show off her bronzed shaven legs, and somehow the view of her tan and toes helps her forget that her pants are work-khaki.

* * *

Nesto makes his final safety checks. He steps out of the car and opens the passenger side door to firmly secure his *abuela* in her seat. He draws the seatbelt across her frail body and maneuvers the straps around her latest *proyecto,* an Aztec-patterned textbook cover "*para sus libros matemáticas y ciencia.*" She is certain he will become "*un doctor.*" *At least* **she** *is certain*, thinks Nesto.

He comes back around to the driver's seat and secures his own safety belt. He makes sure that his Captain America lunch box is braced between the front seats. Any sudden movement could upset the *carne asada* tacos carefully packed inside, and he takes every precaution to avoid such a disaster. He glances one last time at Connie, admiring her steadfast demeanor, and starts the engine. As long as she is settled into the rhythm of her craft, he knows he can, "Do all things."

* * *

In the parking lot, Cathie takes refuge in her mind, tracing the reason she was almost late to work back to her bed. She is grateful for the sanctity of marriage that allows her to… indulge in her passions *and* keep within God's good graces. She thinks about the warmth of her husband's kiss and his skin on hers, because in twelve minutes, surrounded by twenty-four sixth grade math students, these thoughts will be unimaginable.

* * *

Nesto shifts the 1995 Chevy Impala SS into gear, careful not to disturb the shrine to Our Lady of Guadalupe on the dash. At the first stop sign, from beneath the sway of the rosary suspended on the rearview, he checks on Connie. There she sits, ever indifferent. Buoyed up by her stoic confidence in him, he inhales and puts his foot on the gas.

* * *

In the three remaining minutes before the first bell, cars teem in the parking lot. Cathie sighs and looks on at "rush hour." She swirls the last of her coffee in the bottom of her cup and throws it back, taking her eyes momentarily off traffic. *Honestly*, Cathie thinks, *what could I possibly apprehend in the five mile an hour grind?*

The morning light glints off custom chrome rims as a 1995 Chevy Impala SS approaches. The driver's hands are set precisely at ten and two, eyes poised just above the steering wheel. The rosary hanging from the rearview keeps time with the stop and go.

Nesto? Cathie questions.

The car pushes past the drop-off point and makes the tight turn into guest parking. The door opens. The driver exits with a Captain America tin in one hand and these words *"Adiós, Abuela."* On foot, Nesto weaves through the remaining traffic and rises up on the sidewalk.

"Nesto?"

"Buenos días, señora," he starts. Then he realizes his mistake. He slows his speech and says, "Good morning, miss."

Cathie stares back at him blankly.

Nesto contemplates perhaps another more suitable salutation and thinks better of it. He shrugs and turns to go.

"Wait, Nesto. Wait a second. What are you doing?"

"Going to first period, miss?" He punctuates the statement with a question mark because sometimes, with teachers, he reasons, it's hard to know what they want you to say.

42

Cathie doesn't say anything.

So, Nesto gestures toward the car and says, "Oh. You mean Grannie? She's from Mexico. She doesn't drive."

As if that explains everything, he turns to go. Cathie, still speechless, peppers him with silent, indignant questions. Each one evaporates off his Raiders jersey like water droplets on a hot *comal*.

* * *

In the classroom, in the silence that follows attendance and general instruction, Cathie pulls a pink disciplinary referral form from her desk. Her pen searches the boxes for possible offenses: cutting class, excessive tardiness, left grounds without permission, rude, discourteous, excessive talking, unacceptable language, uncooperative. And she discovers it's not there.

She calculates her own tantamount transgressions, skirting the edge of school code and God himself, made manifest in her sandals and her carnal reason for being almost tardy, and she reconsiders.

* * *

On lunch duty in the cafeteria, Cathie scans the crowd. Nesto is cloistered in his posse. Amid the caterwauling confusion of echoed voices in the hall, Cathie closes the space between them. She approaches the lunch table, taking a standing position next to Nesto. Chente, his *compadre*, looks up. He tilts his chin in Cathie's direction, gaining Nesto's attention.

Nesto slides over.

Cathie sits.

He offers her his last taco. *Carne asada con chile verde.*

She leans in and… bites.

And that, Nesto thinks, *is suficiente.*

October: Billy Meets Orlando Bloom

According to The Good Book, the month of October dawns in uncertain times. It's that uncomfortable era between squirrel season and the annual turkey hunt that has Billy Merit gripped with what can only be described as melancholy. It's not that Billy is uncertain of his identity. His name says it all. He stands resolute, "a strong-willed warrior," bolstered by a proud line of Williams that preceded him. And his meretricious homemade trophy collection requires little explanation for Merit. It's these, these uncertain times riding out the vicissitudes of the seasons, where even the leaves change from green to gold, that drives a man to steady himself with time-honored tasks.

* * *

While cleaning his extensive rifle collection in the first rays of morning, his current wife, dressed in a mini-skirt and high heels, enters the living room. With suitcase in tow, she announces: "You never did like change." He doesn't look up, unwilling to face the day, the sound of the wheels rolling across the floor, and whatever else has knocked the shine out of his baby blues.

Indian summer is nature's last call to the brave. Orlando née Orlando Fernàndez gathers himself, drawing his black opaque stockings over his ankles, then his knees, and finally up over his thighs. He forgot to shave. He curses himself for it, one snap decision making this morning's task unnecessarily difficult. He smooths the cotton and Lycra in place, relieving the tiny pinched places here and there, and sighs. His friends call him an evangelist, a bee activist whose passion has him dangling on the edge of sanity. For a moment, a brief moment, Orlando wonders what his enemies think of him. He steps into his costume, tugs on the zipper, and stands in front of the mirror. He checks his stripes, black and yellow, especially the ones leading to the stinger that seems to be more fragile than the rest, and exhales, satisfied.

Squirrels are, no doubt, a menace. And Billy, a man of good character, a man of his word, is not one to shy away from a good fight. A hunter's eye is not given, but earned. Doc, Grannie Max, and other elders of the Valley have told Billy he's a natural. But what they don't understand is Billy is invested.

According to his thorough review of the literature, the state of New Mexico is home to no less than twelve species of squirrel. And, of these, there are five varieties represented in the Black Range mountains, including the tassel-eared, red, rock, thirteen-lined, and golden-mantled ground. While these facts and figures show promise to a trained man's ear, something about the hunt itself is unsatisfying. Pics of Billy dressed in King's Woodland Camo, rodent pelts lashed to his utility belt, tweeted across social media somehow don't measure up—at least not with her.

* * *

It was probably the moment when Orlando announced he officially changed his last name to Bloom that his friends began to doubt him. But he persisted. He persists because colony collapse disorder is not a problem isolated to individuals of the *Apis mellifura* kind. It is the unexaggerated, unadulterated death of us all. *Whatever it takes*, he says to himself, sliding into his rubber boots, *whatever it takes*. In the foyer, Orlando plucks from the coat hook the small basket containing Q-tips. Poised for today's hand pollination, he heads out. Against all odds.

* * *

Billy needs air. There's something about the sound of high heels, roller suitcases, and unadulterated exits that knocks the wind out of him. He selects his favorite Winchester carbine from the lot and heads out. Against all odds.

* * *

Orlando calculates that, due to global warming, he has exactly fourteen and a half days, on the outside, to do what needs to be done. But, in all reality, hoarfrost could descend on any given Sunday, and that would spell disaster for members of the *Asteraceae* family. He can't bear to think of the consequences.

* * *

Billy is bored of his usual targets. He calculates that, on the outside chance that he is found shooting something out of season, the consequences could spell disaster for him and his family. And, he can't bear the thought.

* * *

Orlando feels the pressure of the season mounting. In the resplendent temperatures that characterize Indian summer, he pushes himself to go further today, further afield than ever before.

* * *

Billy shoulders his rifle. He takes a moment, letting the restorative heat of the late season seep into his T-shirt. Despite his best judgment, Billy pushes himself, casting his sights further afield than ever before.

* * *

Orlando senses the unexplained, a divine power, if you will, that manifests in goose bumps, the kind you get when someone's watching over you. With his Q-tip in hand he dabs the precious, fertile golden granules from the male flower and transfers them to female reproductive organs, certain that he feels what can only be described as ecstasy.

* * *

Billy lines up the front and rear combo sights of his rifle. He imagines the ecstatic moment, the golden bullet, if you will, striking the vitals of a tassel-eared specimen, or perhaps a golden-mantled ground. He longs for this moment that can only be described as ecstasy.

* * *

But something is amiss. Everything that Billy thought he knew and understood about the world sandwiched between front and rear combo sights, is blown to smithereens. A confused torrent of yellow and black stripes, Lycra, and rubber strikes his senses in an image that is no less extreme than the theory of global warming itself.

* * *

Orlando startles, a bee caught in Billy's sights. His fear bumbles his words, fragments his sentences, and upsets his punctuation as he searches for whole thoughts. In moments like these, where sense and sensibility prove elusive, Orlando, the brave, extends his hand and offers Billy a Q-tip. "I could use a few good men."

* * *

Billy is dumbfounded. He lowers his rifle to verify the accuracy of his sights. Perhaps his wife is right. Perhaps his perennial aversion to transfiguration has finally pushed him to the brink. Instead of the promised, time-tested accuracy steeled in front and rear vision, Billy finds that this morning is *the* morning. This is the morning when Billy, conscripted by an unforeseen black and yellow foot soldier, picks up a Q-tip to render temerarious abundance for all. And in that same moment, wandering with Orlando among the blooms, he leaves her, dressed in a mini-skirt, standing in the living room of his mind.

November: It's in the Blood

It's been a quiet week in the Mimbres Valley, my home among the singing foothills of the Black Range Mountains. Grannie Max considers the weft and warp of her days and decides that her week has been sanguine. You know, rather upbeat in a season that causes consternation among most folks. From her perch at the Chisme Café she fixes herself the new pour over coffee served at exactly 185 degrees in a glass container, and smiles.

Byron Johnson has never been one for limitations. In utero, Cathie noticed his propensity for heel jabs, testing the limits of her womb, ready for a breakthrough. And yet he does not let go easily, keeping her in labor for sixteen hours with a firm grip on his umbilical cord. When he was twelve, Byron tested the limits of physics with a series of dirt bikes, ramps, and eventually cliffs, managing to flex his tether to gravity itself. And now that he has reached sixteen, Byron seeks new limitations to shatter. He straps his longboard to his backpack, slips into the shoulder straps, and secures the chest buckle. He checks for his goggles perched on the top of his head. They're still there. He opens the front door and exits soundlessly, telling no one of his plans. After all, *were there any?*

He got an early start today—up and dressed by 11 a.m. And for that, he is proud. He pulls his mountain bike to standing and pushes it to the top of the driveway. He looks both ways and laughs. *Have there ever been cars?* He swings his leg over his bike frame and settles his goggles in place, across the bridge of his nose, for the two-mile ride to the paved road.

Nearing Highway 61, Byron is in disbelief. The air is filled with the rare scent of fresh oil on asphalt. He crosses the bridge. And there in the uncertain shade of an errant Siberian elm sapling, he finds her. Clair La Belle. Equipped with her driving gloves, she prepares for the road ahead. She flexes her fingers, awakening the power within. She grips the rims of her wheelchair tires. Byron pulls alongside her. Clair glances up, as if she expected him. Byron stands poised, weight evenly distributed across his pedals and cranks. Backpack secured. Goggles aligned. And at the urging of an inaudible signal, they explode from the starting gates.

The cool November wind cleaved by Clair's hawk nose and Byron's UV-protected, polycarbonate lenses, rushes against ruddy cheeks. The zephyrs glance off Clair's feathered tresses and Byron's tidy bowl updo. The racers dig in, talented athletes in their own rights, bodies honed for sport by the vicissitudes of the road expressed in gravel and asphalt. Hearts pounding, adrenaline pumping. And in the penultimate moment, nearing mile marker 21, the understood finish line, Byron reminds himself of his quest for new. He squeezes his hand brakes, engages the brake cables, and lets

LaBelle fly by. After all, he's never lost before. And that's new.

Efegenia looks on from her charred porch boudoir. She inhales and exhales—pure satisfaction. Wisps of smoke from her Virgin Slim cigarette rise and mingle in the cool. Byron is intrigued. He turns his gaze from Clair's disappearing figure and considers the short distance from the road to Effie's porch, testing new limits. And since his prefrontal cortex is nowhere near developed, in a moment he finds himself perched on the edge of a patio chair on the De la O veranda, asking Effie to light a Slim for him.

"Tough loss," Effie sighs as she slides back into her seat.

Byron glances over at her, unsure exactly how one achieves the satisfaction she finds from her little indulgence, but willing to learn. He inhales like Effie, lower lip heavy with drama and 'Pinky Promise' lipstick. Effie observes him, letting the folds of her silk kimono fall where they may. Byron resists the rising cough as the tobacco burns his throat. Oh, how he wants to exhale—smoothly, the way she does. Instead, he stares straight ahead at nothing in particular, hacks and says, "It wasn't as bad as it looks."

Effie is mysteriously silent. Something about her presence has turned deadly.

Finally, Byron gets the courage to dart his eyes in her direction. He lingers for a moment longer to discover he is this close to being caught—In the claws of a cougar.

* * *

Back out on the road the possibilities ripple. Endless.

He fits his bike tires in the narrow gauge between the double yellow lines of the highway and coasts.

Eyes sheltered from the elements behind rose-tinted alpine lenses,
It's here that man can dream…
It's here that his thoughts can…
Until the relentless adolescent aching in his belly awakens
And he finds himself
At *La Tienda del Sol*
Examining
Hot Cheetos
Doritos

And Eskimo Pies.

* * *

He makes his way to the refrigerated cases for a cream soda.

"Does your ma know you're drinkin'?" Doc challenges. He doubts everyone, priding himself today as a voice of reason echoing across Byron's hormonal sea. Byron bristles.

"Ah, quit yer gripin'," Lester calls out. "Make him a caramel frappe. Double shot."

"And slide over, Judd. Make some room for the man. This is Brandon's boy." Judd grips his mocha with extra whip, slides over a bit on the red vinyl booth seat, and offers Byron the warm spot.

Byron is skeptical at first. *Why all the sudden attention?* He reaches up, checks for his goggles. They're still there—rose-colored and all. He shrugs. Byron isn't one to turn down a drink if someone's buying, so he sits.

"As I was sayin'," Norman starts, settling into conversational rhythms, tried and true. "I think we oughtta help her get into office."

Byron vaguely recognizes that revolutionary gleam in Norman's eyes.

"Who? Sarah Palin?" Lester asks.

"Yep."

"There's only one room in the House I'd like to see that woman in," Lester sneers, "and it ain't the office."

"Aw, come on, Lester," Norman reasons. "You got like one track in that mind of yers."

"Two," Lester says rubbing a hand over his belly.

Norman ignores him. "I mean Sarah Palin in office could be magic!" Norman breathes with stars in his eyes.

"Does your wife know about this?" Judd enjoins with a laugh.

Judd's remark forces Norm back in his "man cave." Realizing that he's lost control of himself, he puts on the proper front for a man of his stature. Losing control is something one doesn't do, even if it's for a minute. Norman's voice deepens.

"I'm just sayin' that we could really get some traction on the things that matter to us—second amendment rights and keeping the west free. I mean, are you really gonna let these radicals run the place? Pass the effing salt."

In that moment, Byron discovers the one limitation he has never shattered.

51

Being Home

Riveted to the red vinyl seating with the dregs of his caramel frappe, Byron can barely contain himself.

"Are you in a hurry, son?" Lester inquires.

"You really should'na given him a double," Judd admonishes.

Byron can't answer. The last of the whipped cream rides up the inside of his straw and rolls across his tongue. And then he's gone.

Byron arrives home in time for dinner—wild rice, flounder, steamed greens. Grannie Max is in attendance. His mom has worked on several campaigns with her: Save the Minnow, Hug a Wolf, Free the Nipple, or something. He takes his seat next to his sister, passing the platters, the water jug, the salt, the pepper. He considers his father at one end of the pine-top oval table, then his mother at the other. He looks up at Grannie Max, a woman so jolly and almost elfin with the sparkle in her eye. He feels what he has always felt at home—loved. He inhales and prepares himself for what's next.

And on the exhalation he says, "Pass the effing butter."

The whole table is quiet. Byron knows he has done it. He has ventured into unknown territory. The silence that ensues is heavy, palpable, almost oppressive.

"Congratulations," Grannie Max finally says with a giggle. "You've raised a fine young man. And a good looking one, too."

December: As the Raven Flies

Tio Chancho emerges from his Man Cave. It is time. In the past few weeks, he has watched Colts vs. Ravens, Lions vs. Bengals, Dolphins vs. Bears. And he realizes they are all the same. He has never betrayed his growing sense of melancholia to his Man Tribe. But he knows it has gone too far. Today, he found himself enthralled by a televised Olympic curling match. He has to come clean. He knows it. But not now. He shades his eyes from the weak winter sun, translucent in the morning sky. He brushes Dorito dust from his Dolphins jersey, hitches up his plaid pajama pants, and descends the porch stairs. He strides the ten paces to the plastic form of baby Jesus in the yard, searches for the cord, and plugs it in.

    A meander. That's what he tries to tell himself it was. *A harmless meander on the channels*. But it wasn't. And, deep down, he knows it.

* * *

Orlando stands on the threshold of the closet. He knows he has to do it. He bunches up the dry cleaning bag, feeds the neck of the hanger through the top hole and smooths the plastic over his bee suit. It is time. The past few months have been full of warm spells, here and there, inviting an extended pollination season. But, in the end, Orlando knows winter will win. It always does. He places the bee suit in its rightful place between his leprechaun suit and his Santa suit and sighs. Bee season is his favorite, but you can't halt the march of time.

* * *

Tia Maria straightens the heart-shaped *ristra* on her door and prepares herself. Tonight *la familia* will gather. She anticipates Chancho's incessant talk of football, Orlando's strange silences, the *tias*, the *primos*, and *Abuela*—the one who knits them all together, literally. Maria hopes *Abuela* will bring Nesto. They worry about him. On the porch picnic table, Maria straddles the bench. She hears the rustle of raven feathers as one alights on the power pole. She continues to fill brown paper bags with sand. She sets the votive candles in and among the coarse grains, careful not to scratch her scarlet manicure. *Luminarias*, she thinks. *Perfect for tonight's forecast—clear with a chance of meteor showers.*

    Nesto rises early. It is time. According to the calendar of holy days, today dawns after *Día de la Virgen de Guadalupe*, but before Christmas. Today is the day the Lord has made, the day every year when his *abuela* needs him. He puts on paint-splattered jeans, an old Raider's jersey, and pulls up his socks. He scrubs clean the watering trough in the backyard, opens the packages of cornhusks, and dowses them in boiling water.

* * *

Byron lifts his rose-colored ski goggles. He feels the rush and wheel of black wing beats overhead. He pays homage with 1… 2… 3 seconds of his attention. He goes back to scrolling Instagram from the tailgate of his daddy's truck. He counts his "Likes," his "Followers," his "Posts," and is dissatisfied. It's all the same.

"Sweetie," he hears his mom call to his dad from the kitchen. "Are we really gonna keep this Kombucha for another year? It honestly keeps me up at night. I'm afraid it's going to escape the jar. What will the neighbors think?" she jokes.

And then the conversation heads south, like really south as it always does, when his dad tries to convince his mom of anything, and they think the kids are outside.

Angela climbs up on the tailgate with Byron and sighs.

"I know what you're getting for Christmas," he says. Then, he thinks better of it. He knows better. He turns to look at Angela and decides now is not the time to ruin Christmas. As a truce or a kind of peace offering, he says, "Dad says you'll like it. I think it's weird."

Angela changes the subject. "Wanna play in the tree house?"

Byron considers his age… sixteen, his shoe size… eleven-and-a-half, and the fact that older brothers are not designed to like little sisters, and he relents. "Ok. Just this once."

* * *

Grannie Max sweeps the porch. The morning light bounces off crystals clinging to the corn stalks. She smiles to herself, heart lifted by the evening ahead. Earlier this week, she told Defenders of Wildlife, Wild Women of the West, and her Stitch and Bitch Club that she couldn't make the holiday parties. Mennonite Mary raised an eyebrow, but kept it to herself. She knows Grannie hasn't been sick in thirty years. But she also knows when to keep information like that close to her chest.

Eddie wished *Feliz Navidad* to family, friends, and neighbors early this year. His prayers to God were finally answered. Eddie knows Jesus is enough. And finally, Eddie knows he is more than adequate for Grannie Max. For that, Eddie gives praise. He mounts the front porch steps.

"*Hola, señor,*" Grannie Max breathes after their kiss.

"*Hola, mi amor.*"

Yes, Eddie has made it. Crossing the threshold of the home of Maxine DeNeuve with his size seven sneakers—Eddie has made it.

* * *

From her nest within the swing and sway of the sycamore branches, Raven considers her assets. Standing on the edge of the deep bowl of branches lined with roots, mud and bark, she relishes in treasures gleaned from her territory. It is laid out before her like pages of a calendar. In February, she wove kitten fur plucked from the frozen highway. Then there was lint and a cigarette butt. By May, a *tamarindo* wrapper gleamed, followed by the stiff yellow fibers of twine that once hung from a trailer ball. There was the curious "I voted" sticker that clung to her feathers worse than mud ever did. And then there was the matchstick—red hot. There were scraps of yarn found in the school parking lot. And then there was a Q-tip. Today, Raven found a shred of cornhusk wrapper, emptied of its delectable contents.

As the last rays fade from the sky, Raven adjusts herself, bedding down for the night. She strategizes the best sleeping position, sheltered from falling meteors and out of the glare of baby Jesus. She revels in the peace found among the branches, beneath the weight of the winter night sky.

57

About the Author

Catalina Claussen

Catalina Claussen is an award-winning young adult novelist, poet, and short story author who carries on a love affair with the land, language, and people of southwest New Mexico. She lives with her daughter, 3 dogs, and a prolific garden on a ranch in the Mimbres Valley.

Her two young adult novels *Diamonds at Dusk* (2016) and *Diamonds at Dawn* (2018), have been recognized by the Arizona/New Mexico Book Awards, The Wishing Shelf Book Awards in the United Kingdom, and the New Apple Book Awards for Excellence in Independent Publishing.

Being Home is her debut short story collection. To listen to the podcasts of the stories included in this book, go to the author's website at catalinaclaussenbooks.wordpress.com.

About the Photographer

Ajalaa Claussen

Ajalaa Claussen is a recent graduate from Aldo Leopold Charter School in Silver City, NM. As the daughter of Catalina Claussen, she was raised in the Mimbres Valley surrounded by an extended family of writers and photographers. This collection of photographs showcases her artistic progression from the age of 10-18. The stories share bits and pieces of her childhood, as she literally grew up on these pages.

Her work has been exhibited at the McCray Gallery on the Western New Mexico University campus, Javalina Coffeehouse, and the Bayard Public Library. This fall she will attend the University of Southern California to study political science and media studies.

Progressive Rising Phoenix Press is an independent publisher. We offer wholesale pricing and multiple binding options with no minimum purchases for schools, libraries, book clubs, and retail vendors. We offer substantial discounts on bulk orders and discounts on individual sales through our online store. Please visit our website at:

www.ProgressiveRisingPhoenix.com

*If you enjoyed reading this book, please review it on Amazon, B & N, or Goodreads.
Thank you in advance!*